MONSTER BUDDIES

I'M ALL WRAPPED UP!

MEET A MUMMY

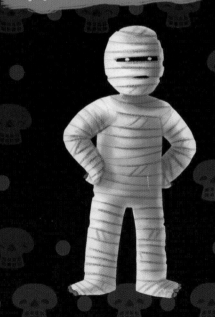

Shannon Knudsen

illustrated by **Renée Kurilla**

M MILLBROOK PRESS • MINNEAPOLIS

For Mama, the most wonderful mummy ever –SK

For LV and Maggie, two kiddos that could
outsmart a mummy in their sleep!
–RK

Millbrook Press
A division of Lerner Publishing Group, Inc.
241 First Avenue North
Minneapolis, MN 55401 USA

For reading levels and more information, look up this title at www.lernerbooks.com.

Main body text set in Sunshine Regular 17/24.
Typeface provided by Chank.

Library of Congress Cataloging-in-Publication Data

Knudsen, Shannon, 1971–
    I'm all wrapped up! Meet a mummy / by Shannon Knudsen.
      pages   cm. — (Monster buddies)
    ISBN 978-0-7613-9188-3 (lib. bdg. : alk. paper)
    ISBN 978-1-4677-4779-0 (eBook)
    1. Mummies—Juvenile literature. I. Title.
  GN293.K68 2015
  393'.3—dc23   2013037349

Manufactured in the United States of America
1 – BOL – 7/15/14

TABLE OF CONTENTS

Hello, Mummy!

SMASH! CRASH! Yikes, something just broke down the door! It looks like a person, but it's covered in cloth. What is this thing?!

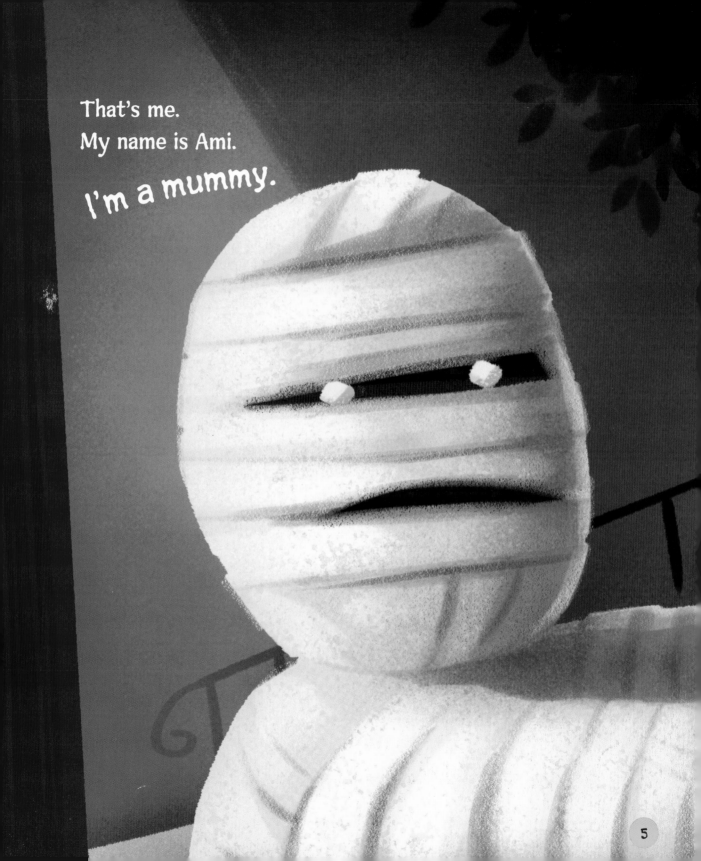

That's me.
My name is Ami.
I'm a mummy.

The Real Deal with Mummies

You probably know lots of monster stories. And you probably know that monsters aren't real.

But mummies *are* real. Sort of. You even might see a real mummy one day. But it won't be walking down the street. It will be stuck behind glass in a museum.

Museum mummies won't break that glass. They won't even get up. What about my kind of mummy—the monster kind?

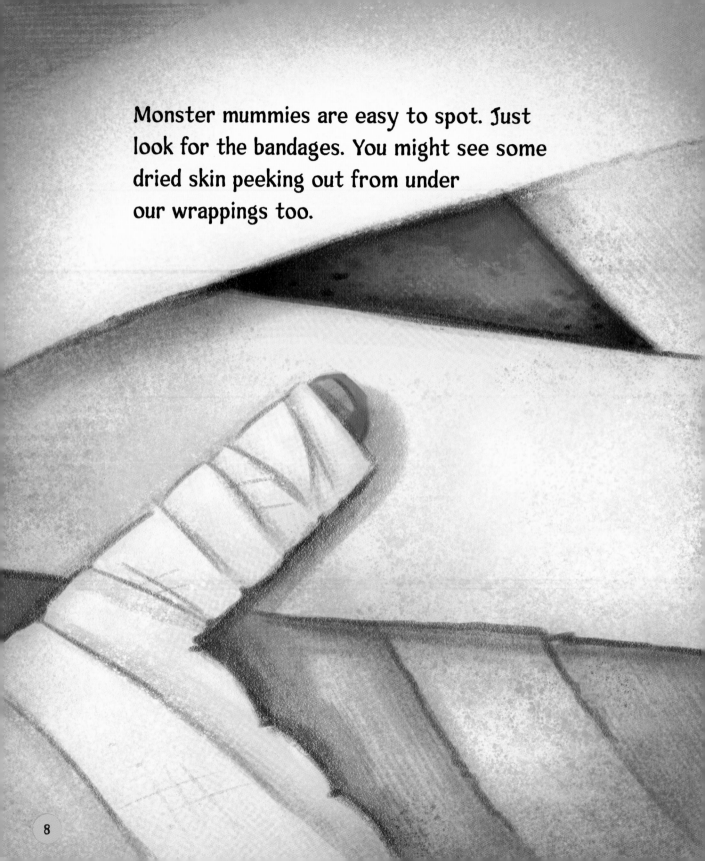

Monster mummies are easy to spot. Just
look for the bandages. You might see some
dried skin peeking out from under
our wrappings too.

Mummies can't run. Some of us can barely walk! That's because our bodies are stiff. Sometimes we hold our arms straight out to stay balanced.

If a mummy ever comes after you,
watch out! Mummies can bash through
walls. We may be slow, but we never
give up a chase. We don't even stop
to eat or sleep.

Mummies are tough to fight too. Fire can slow us down for a while. But if a mummy chases you, your best bet is to run.

And then run some more!

How to Make a Mummy

Thousands of years ago, I lived as a rich lady in Egypt. Lucky for me, rich people who died were made into mummies. My religion taught people that becoming a mummy would keep my body safe. That way, I would reach the next life unharmed.

After I died, a priest took out the soft parts of my body. Then he used salt to dry my body. Finally, he wrapped me in cloth. All that work took seventy days! To finish the job, the priest placed a painted mask over my face.

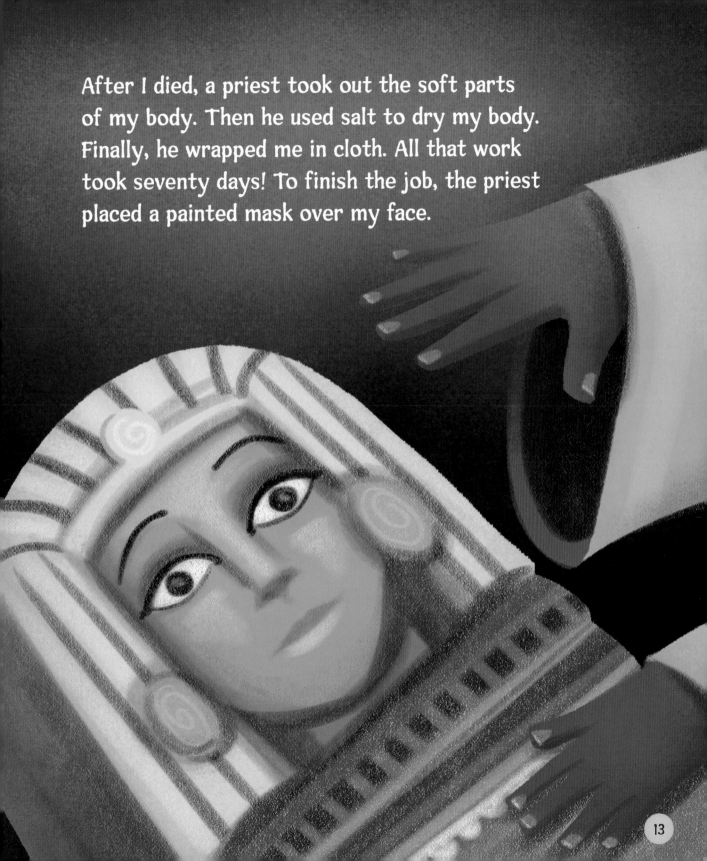

I lay in a fancy stone box called a sarcophagus. Servants carried my sarcophagus into a secret tomb. My servants put my gold and jewels in the tomb. They wanted to be sure I would be rich forever. They brought food too. And they painted the walls of the tomb with scenes from my life.

Back to Life!

My tomb was a lovely place. So lovely that many years later, a gang of nasty thieves broke in. They were hoping to steal my gold. One of them found a scroll with special writing on it. The thief read the words out loud. What a mistake!

Those words brought me back to life.

I climbed right out of my sarcophagus. Oh, the look of surprise on the thief's face! He didn't get very far before I caught him.

Ever since that day, I've been hunting the rest of that gang. I hate being away from my tomb, but I need to teach those thieves a lesson. I even put a curse on them. No one who breaks into my tomb will live to tell the tale!

Wrapping It Up

Now you know the truth about mummies, from our bandages to our tombs. And when you see a mummy in a museum, you'll know it won't come to life. It won't put a curse on you. It won't even move.

Wait . . . did you see that?

A Mummy's Day Writing Activity

You've learned a lot about mummies. Now you're ready to spin a spooky tale of your own. Grab a pencil and a piece of paper. Write a short story about what a mummy's day is like. Does it chase thieves? Does it hang out with other mummies? Draw a picture to go with your story.

GLOSSARY

bandages: strips of cloth wrapped around a mummy

curse: a set of magical words that cause harm or trouble

mummy: a dead body that has been dried out

sarcophagus: a stone box that holds a dead body

scroll: a roll of paper or animal skin with writing on it

tomb: a building or room where a dead body is kept

TO LEARN MORE

Books

Doeden, Matt. *Tools and Treasures of Ancient Egypt.* Minneapolis: Lerner Publications, 2014.
Check out this book to learn what life was like for the people of ancient Egypt.

Rex, Michael. *The Runaway Mummy: A Petrifying Parody.* New York: Putnam Books for Young Readers, 2012.
A young mummy learns that his mother will protect him even if he runs away in this tribute to the classic children's book *The Runaway Bunny.*

Websites

The Mummy Countdown
http://www.schoolsliaison.org.uk/kids/egyptmummy.htm
Solve nine clues about mummies and their tombs to reveal a mummy from Egypt!

Tomb of the Unknown Mummy
http://kids.nationalgeographic.com/kids/games/interactiveadventures/tomb-unknown-mummy/
Use your lantern to find all the artifacts in the mummy's tomb before time runs out!

INDEX